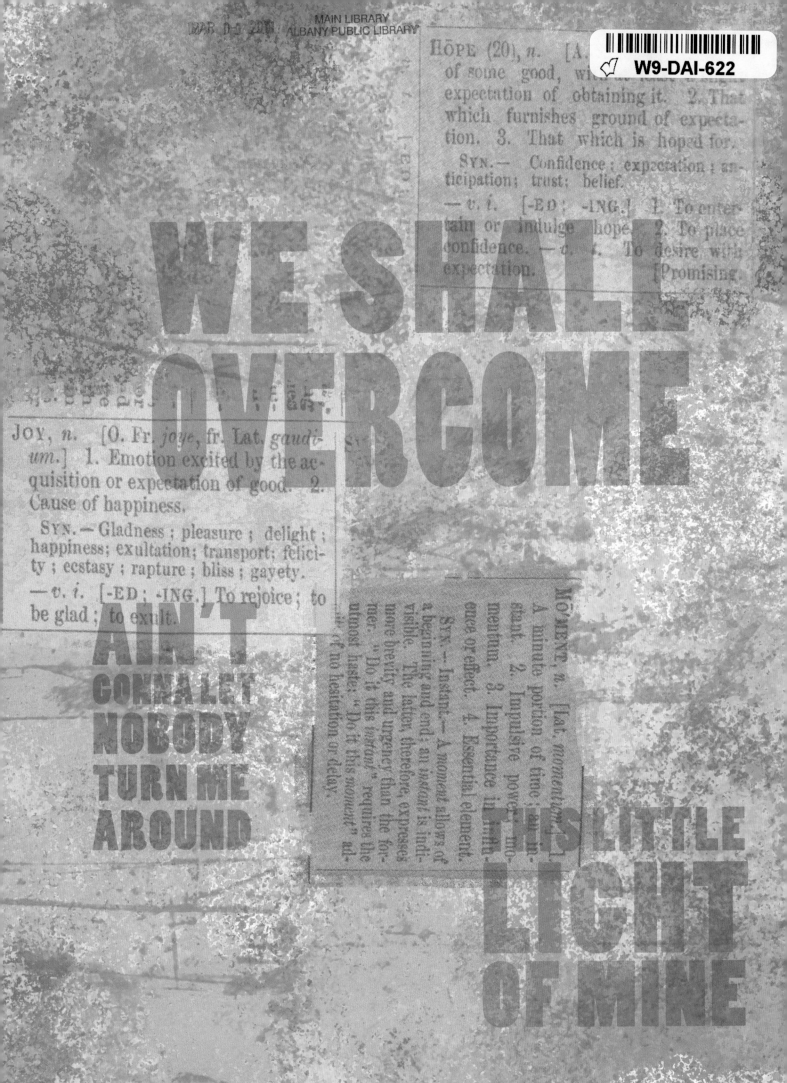

This book is dedicated to all the beautiful souls that I call family and friends who let their lights shine daily.

To Lori, Harriet, Elliot, and Karen, thank you from the bottom of my heart.   --V.N.

Published in the United States 2009 by

🍎 Blue Apple Books

515 Valley Street, Maplewood, NJ 07040

www.blueapplebooks.com

Distributed in the U.S. by Chronicle Books

First Edition   Printed in China

ISBN: 978-1-934706-90-9

10 9 8 7 6 5 4 3 2 1

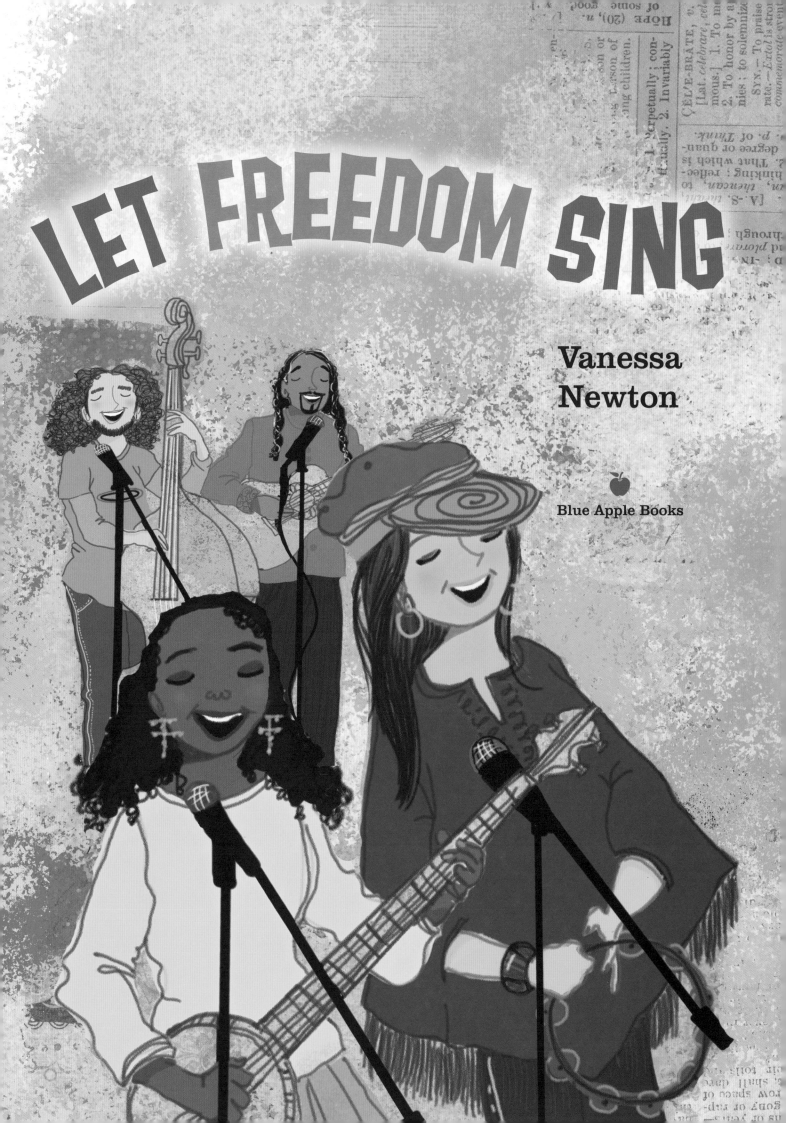

FREEDOM SINGS!

Powerful. Inspirational. Unifying. Music was an undeniable force in the Civil Rights movement in the 1950's and 1960's. At marches, at meetings, at demonstrations, songs motivated activists who were expressing their desire for freedom and equality. Many of the protest songs were African-American spirituals, their lyrics adapted to speak about the hardships black Americans faced day in, day out.

Again and again these songs were sung—in Montgomery, Greensboro, Little Rock, New Orleans, Selma, and Washington, D.C.—all over the South where scores of people gathered, fighting for change.

They sang about boycotting buses...

If you miss me at the back of the bus
If you can't find me back there
Come on up to the front of the bus
I'll be sittin right there

sitting at lunch counters...

I'm gonna sit at the Woolworth counter,
I'm gonna sit at the Woolworth counter one of these days

marching for equal rights...

Will you march for your rights?
"Certainly, Lord."
Will you march for your rights?
"Certainly, Lord."

serving time in jail...

Ain't gonna let no jailhouse
Turn me 'roun
I'm gonna keep on walkin'
Keep on talkin'
Walkin' into freedom land

attending school...

If you can't find me in the school room
If you can't find me in there
Come on out to the picket line
I'll be standing right there

standing ground...

We're fighting for our rights and
We shall not be moved
Just like a tree that's planted by the water,
We shall not be moved

overcoming all odds...

We shall overcome,
We shall overcome
We shall overcome someday
Oh-o deep in my heart
I do believe
We shall overcome someday

and letting the best in themselves shine the brightest...

This little light of mine,
I'm going to let it shine.
Let it shine, let it shine, let it shine.

This Little Light of Mine captured the spirit and heart of the movement. A gospel children's song written by Harry Dixon Loes, it became an anthem of the time thanks to the efforts of civil rights activists Zilphia Horton and Fannie Lou Hamer.

* If You Miss Me at the Back of the Bus; I'm Gonna Sit at the Welcome Table; Certainly Lord; Ain't Gonna Let Nobody Turn Me 'Round; If You Miss Me at the Back of the Bus; We Shall Not be Moved; We Shall Overcome; This Little Light of Mine

Confronted with dehumanizing indignities and daily sacrifices, each person had to find their inner strength and resolve – their inner light.

Rosa Parks did.

Dr. Martin Luther King, Jr. did.

Ernest Green did.

Elizabeth Eckford did.

Jefferson Thomas did.

Terrence Roberts did.

Carlotta Walls did.

Minnijean Brown did.

Gloria Ray did.

Thelma Mothershed did.

Melba Pattillo did.

Ezell A. Blair Jr. did.

David Richmond did.

Joseph McNeil did.

Franklin McCain did.

Ruby Bridges did.

Lyndon B. Johnson did.

Barack Obama did.

They and many others, unnamed and unsung, let their lights shine.

From the editors at Blue Apple Books

This little light of mine,

I'm gonna let it shine.

This little light of mine,
I'm going to let it shine.

This little light of mine,
I'm going to let it shine.

Let it shine!

Let it shine!

Let it shine!

On benches just for 'colored,'
Black folks obeyed the rules.

DECEMBER 1, 1955

Rosa Parks refused to move,
She let her light shine.

Preaching from his pulpit,
Dr. King had a dream.

When he spoke in Alabama,
He let his light shine.

DECEMBER 4,
1955

BUS STOP

DECEMBER 5, 1955

DECEMBER 21, 1956

With boycotts in Montgomery,
Dr. King inspired all.

Walkers along the bus routes,
They let their lights shine.

This little light of mine,
I'm going to let it shine.

This little light of mine,
I'm going to let it shine.

This little light of mine,
I'm going to let it shine.

Let it shine!

Let it shine!

Let it shine!

SEPTEMBER 23, 1957

The Little Rock Nine:
Ernest Green, Elizabeth Eckford,
Jefferson Thomas, Gloria Ray,
Terrence Roberts, Carlotta Walls,
Minnijean Brown, Melba Pattillo,
Thelma Mothershed.

Schools for blacks in Little Rock,
Separate, but not equal.

Nine high school kids,
They let their lights shine.

Students at lunch counters—
They hoped to be served.

As the Greensboro Four sat waiting,
They let their lights shine.

At a school in New Orleans,
Shouting filled the air.

Ruby Bridges walked alone.
She let her light shine.

This little light of mine,
I'm going to let it shine.

This little light of mine,
I'm going to let it shine.

This little light of mine,
I'm going to let it shine.

Let it shine!

Let it shine!

Let it shine!

AUGUST 28, 1963

At the March on Washington,
Thousands walked for miles.

Dr. King had a dream.
He let his light shine.

President Lyndon Johnson
Helped to change the law.

JULY 2, 1964

—

AUGUST 6, 1965

Civil rights for everyone.
He let his light shine.

JANUARY 20, 2009

Speaking to all Americans,
Barack Obama had a dream.

As President of the United States,
He let his light shine.

This little light of mine,
I'm going to let it shine.

This little light of mine,
I'm going to let it shine.

This little light of mine,
I'm going to let it shine.

Let it SHINE!

I'M GONNA SIT AT THE WELCOME TABLE

CERTAINLY LORD

WE SHALL NOT BE MOVED

IF YOU MISS ME AT THE BACK OF THE BUS